Unflappable
Matthew Ward & Scott Magoon

Clarion Books
An Imprint of HarperCollinsPublishers

We are birds.

But we are not like most birds.
Although we have wings...

we do not fly.

Yet.

We are

working

on it.

We train every day.

We dream.

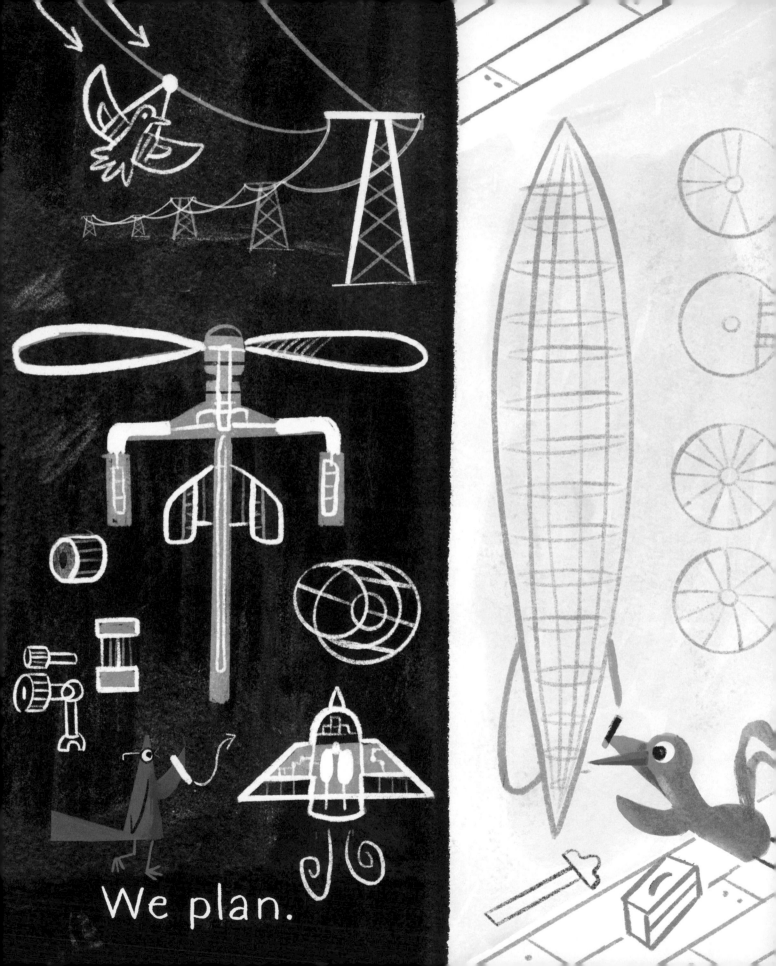

We plan.

We build.

Someday we will fly.

But flying is hard.

Sometimes we do not measure right.

Sometimes

our

bubbles

burst.

Sometimes . . .

things

just

go

wrong.

Sometimes we fall down.

Sometimes we want
to give up.

But giving up is for worms.

We are not worms.

We are birds.

We do not give up.

It might

not be

today.

It might
not be next
Tuesday.

fly.

we will

Oh. It IS today.
We are flying now.

Good-bye.

For my three big little birds. If ever you have
trouble flying, never stop trying. —M.W.

For my friends at Clarion and HMH. Past,
present, and future. Birds of a feather. —S.M.

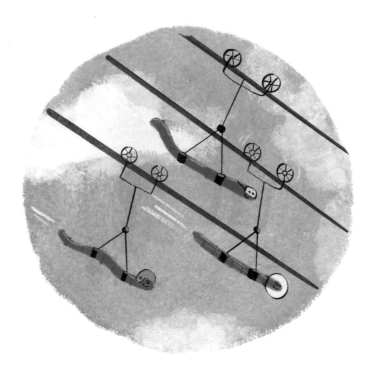

Clarion Books is an imprint of HarperCollins Publishers.

Unflappable
Text copyright © 2023 by Matthew Ward
Illustrations copyright © 2023 by Scott Magoon

Library of Congress Control Number: 2022049068
ISBN 978-0-35-840005-9

The artist used Procreate, iPad, and Apple Pencil to create the digital illustrations for this book.
Hand lettering by Scott Magoon
Typography by Whitney Leader-Picone
23 24 25 26 27 RTLO 10 9 8 7 6 5 4 3 2 1

First Edition